Quentin Blake

Three Little Monkeys at Christmas

ILLUSTRATED BY
Emma Chichester Clark

HarperCollins *Children's Books*

First published in hardback in Great Britain by HarperCollins *Children's Books* in 2021

1 3 5 7 9 10 8 6 4 2

ISBN: 978–0–00–835792–4

HarperCollins *Children's Books* is a division of HarperCollins*Publishers* Ltd
1 London Bridge Street, London SE1 9GF

www.harpercollins.co.uk

HarperCollins*Publishers*, 1st Floor, Watermarque Building, Ringsend Road, Dublin 4, Ireland

Printed and bound in Italy

Hilda Stibbs was going to stay with her Uncle Gilbert for Christmas.
With her were her three little monkeys, Tim and Sam and Lulu.

"He lives in the lap of luxury," said Hilda. "But it will be more
enjoyable for him not to have to spend Christmas on his own."

Uncle Gilbert lived in a large flat at the top of a grand building in the city.

His flat was full of **amazing** things.

There were all kinds of statues and vases, furniture and
extraordinary clocks, and a cut-glass model of the Eiffel Tower.

But the most amazing thing was his prized possession,
the **Golden Teapot**. It was solid gold and had
been made in China two thousand years ago.

"I'm always afraid someone will try to steal it," said Uncle Gilbert. "But I do like to have it here to admire."

The next morning Hilda said it was important that they should have a real traditional Christmas, and they should go and buy a Christmas tree.

"You must be very good while we're away," she said to her little monkeys.

But the little monkeys soon began to get bored.

They
climbed
into
the
vases.

They rolled them
up and down
the floor.

They danced with the
cups and saucers.

Hilda and her Uncle Gilbert came back
home with a **beautiful** Christmas tree.

It even had a fairy on top.

But when they opened the
door, what did they see?

"You naughty little
monkeys," said Hilda.
"Why did I bring you
away for Christmas?"

Tim and Sam and
Lulu looked at her
with their big round
eyes and said nothing.

The next morning Hilda and
Uncle Gilbert went out again.

Hilda said, "We must get a big box of
Christmas crackers and some hooters
and some party hats. Christmas isn't
Christmas without party hats."

She looked at the little monkeys.
"And you must be very good
while we are away."

But the little monkeys
very soon began to get bored.

They opened the drawers
and threw out Uncle Gilbert's
shirts and ties and socks.

They opened the shoe cupboard
and threw out the shoes
and tied the shoelaces together.

They pulled off all the lampshades.

When Hilda and Uncle Gilbert got back with their box of Christmas crackers, what did they see?

Hilda said, "You naughty little monkeys. I should never have brought you away for Christmas."

Tim and Sam and
Lulu looked at her
with their big round
eyes and said nothing.

That afternoon Hilda and her Uncle Gilbert went out once again.

Hilda said, "For it to be a real Christmas, we must have holly and mistletoe. And, Tim and Sam and Lulu, you must be **very good** while we're out."

But the little monkeys soon began to get bored.

They ate the crackers,

they blew on the hooters

and they tried on
the paper hats.

When Hilda and Uncle Gilbert came
back with their holly and mistletoe,
what did they see?

Hilda said, "You naughty little
monkeys! Whatever made me bring
you with me for Christmas?"

Tim and Sam and Lulu looked at her with
their big round eyes and said nothing.

Later that afternoon
Hilda and Uncle Gilbert
went out again.

"All we need now," said Hilda,
"are some lovely presents. Christmas
is nothing without presents."

"And this time,"
she said to the
little monkeys,

"you must be

very

good

indeed."

It was already getting dark, so they did not see a sinister figure on the roof above Uncle Gilbert's flat.

When Hilda and Uncle Gilbert came up the front steps with their arms full of presents,

Hilda said, "I do hope those little monkeys have not been naughty again."

But when they opened the door of the flat, what did they see?

There in front of
them was a man
completely tied
up in the Christmas
decorations.

There was holly in his beard,
hooters in his ears,
the fairy was on top of his head
and he was holding the
Golden Teapot.

When the police came, they said, "This is Oscar Mogg, the international art thief.

We have never been able to catch him in the act,

but now these three little monkeys have done the job for us."

They shook hands with each of the monkeys.

As the police officer took Oscar Mogg away, Uncle Gilbert said, "Perhaps now we can sit down and relax after all the excitement."

Hilda said, "You wonderful little monkeys."

They went into the
sitting room and when
they got there Uncle
Gilbert nearly **fainted**.

But that is the sort of thing you have to expect if you are going
to invite three little monkeys to stay with you at Christmas.